THE DISCOVERY OF THE NATIONS

VIOLENCE IS NOT THE KEY

THE DISCOVERY OF THE NATIONS
A SHORT STORY BY MALIK MURPHY

VIOLENCE IS NOT THE KEY
A POEM BY MALIK MURPHY

The Discovery of the Nations (Short Story)
Violence is Not the Key (Poem)
© 2025 Malik Murphy
Cover Art © 2025 Malik Murphy
ISBN: 979-8-9987811-7-9

Published by Youth Writer's Press
Colton, California
youthwriterspress.com

First Edition, 2025

To request permissions, you may contact the Publisher at
info@youthwriterscamp.com

Printed in the United States of America.

Cover design by Malik Murphy & Emily Anne Evans
Layout design by Emily Anne Evans / Photon Moment LLC

CONTENTS

FOREWORD

It is with great pride and admiration that I introduce *The Discovery of the Nations*, the debut work of my son, Malik Murphy. At just eleven years old, Malik has written a story that blends action, imagination, and purpose. What makes this book so special is not only the thrilling adventure of young friends turned heroes but also the heart and values woven into every page.

Malik's story shows us the importance of courage, teamwork, and doing what is right—even when it's not easy. His characters remind us that true leadership is about serving others and lifting up those who face challenges. In a time when our communities need positive examples, Malik has offered us a tale that inspires hope and possibility.

This book is more than an adventure. It is a reflection of Malik's own passion for helping others and his belief that everyone has the power to make a difference. I believe readers of all ages will find themselves entertained, inspired, and encouraged to be the best version of themselves.

The Discovery of the Nations is the beginning of Malik Murphy's journey as both a writer and a leader. I am honored to witness and support the start of what promises to be a remarkable path ahead.

— Minyan Murphy

THE DISCOVERY OF THE NATIONS

There was a kid named David, who lived in Texas. They say everything is bigger in Texas, including David's bed where he loves to sleep and dream about becoming a spy.

One morning, he woke up and ate breakfast before getting on the bus and going to his first day of middle school.

As he was entering the classroom door, he bumped into two kids named Eric and Angela and fell to the floor. Eric and Angela were courteous and helped him up. David felt grateful to encounter two nice kids on his first day of school.

During lunch, Eric and Angela invited David to sit at their table. Angela asked David how was he enjoying his first day of school.

He replied, "It's going really well so far, but how did you two meet each other?"

Erica and Angela laughed. Eric said, "We are siblings."

Angela asked David if he had any siblings.

David replied, "No, I just have my dog Kofi."

DAVID

The bell just rang, and it was time for me to find my bus to get back home. Lost in the crowd of students, I find myself encountering Angela and Eric getting on the same bus as me. *I didn't know we lived in the same neighborhood,* I thought to myself.

As I found my seat next to them, Eric said "I didn't know we were riding on the same bus."

I answer back, "What street do you guys live on?"

Eric responds, "Barnie Ave."

"I live on Crossboard St., which is the next street over." At least I have friends to walk home with in this sketchy neighborhood.

When we all got off the bus, we witnessed a guy breaking into someone's house. We all got scared and ran to our homes. When I made it inside, I went up the stairs to FaceTime Eric and Angela.

Angela said, "Only if I was more skilled at kung fu, I would have stopped that guy."

Eric follows her statement and says, "Yeah if only I was better at wrestling we would have gotten that guy."

"You two have quite the skills," I reply.

Together Eric and Angela asked, "What is your skill, David?"

"My skill is working with technology," I say. "I really hate the crime that has been happening in our community, it makes me feel horrible."

Eric replies, "Me too, bro."

The following day, Angela had kung fu practice. I wanted to see how good she was, so I asked my mom if I could go.

When we arrived, practice had just begun. They started stretching and working on their form. They then practiced punching on boards, and she hit the record of breaking ten boards at once. Dang!

"She's really good at this," I told Eric. Eric said, "If we keep improving our skills we can become spies of the nations and stop criminals worldwide."

Heck yeah, that's my ultimate dream and we have the perfect dream team.

ANGELA

"Guys I never broke ten boards before, did you see that?"

Eric said, "Yeah that's your new personal record."

After my water break, we began working on our kicks. Out of the whole class, I had the best kicks, even my Sifu agreed.

When class ended, we decided to have a sleepover at David's house. Little did we know, this was a journey of becoming our spy dream team.

Years passed, and Eric, Angela, and David continued to be friends. They end up going to the same high school and even college!

One day, they all went out bowling for David's birthday. He is celebrating his twenty-second birthday and their 10 years of friendship. Even at this age, they still desire to discover and be the spies of the nations.

DAVID

As soon as we got back to my house from bowling, which is on the same street I grew up on, I decided to have a conversation with Eric and Angela.

"The reason why I invited you both over is because... well, it sounds like a really crazy idea especially now that we are adults; but what if we became..."

Eric interjects and blurts out, "Don't tell me what I think you're going to say."

"Spies!" I yell.

Eric replies, "Agh, I knew you were going to say that."

ERIC

While sitting on the couch, I was thinking *it's been a while since Angela and I spoke to David. I wonder if he forgot about our last conversation of becoming spies.* I turned on the TV to watch the news and they are reporting how there was a robbery at JP Morgan Bank.

I called David and he finally answered his phone. "Bro! Where have you been, we have not heard from you."

David said, "Just come to my house and I'll tell you about everything."

DAVID

When they arrived, I took them to my basement.

Eric said, "OMG David what is all of this."

"These are the suits and gadgets. Eric, this one is yours; it's my product called Gripper Gloves. These gloves can stick to high frequency metals and buildings. This will allow you to be able to climb tall buildings. And according to my calculations, it's only a 0.17% chance of falling."

"So, Angela, are you ready for yours?" I say.

She said, "Yep."

"This is my product called Absorb Balls. These metal balls will allow you to absorb any negative energy. For example, when you are coming in contact or battle with a negative person tap the red button on the ball and you'll be able to suction them into the absorb ball. The only way this will work is if the person is laying down."

I then say, "With the combination of my technology, Angela's kung fu and Eric's wrestling skills we should have what it takes to defeat gangs across the nations."

ERIC

"Guys, on the news earlier, right before David called me, they were talking about how a gang was robbing a big bank."

"Maybe we can use the gadgets that David provided to go out and stop this robbery. Let's first make a plan to analyze how many robbers are involved," I say. "David, do you think you can handle this?"

David replies, "I am already on it bro."

Angela says, "We can take my car to the scene." She proceeds to ask David for the location of the bank robbery.

David replies, "the location has been sent to both of your phones."

DAVID

We discussed our plan to put a stop to the bank robbery in our community and are now moving forward to execute our agenda of becoming spies.

There are five bank robbers, and they have twenty-three hostages held inside. Our mission is to save each one of the hostages and escort the robbers to jail.

As Eric and Angela are on the way to the crime scene, I am handling the tech behind the scenes and ordering me a pepperoni pizza. Besides, I can't handle all this crime on an empty stomach.

ANGELA

My brother and I made it to JP Morgan Bank but decided to enter from the back.

First, I went to take out the closest guy next to me. I went for a simple kick towards the face, made contact and he fell onto the ground. One of the other robbers noticed me by how hard the guy fell to the floor and started to shoot in my direction. Luckily, I escaped in time to dodge the bullets.

Eric went for a tackle by grabbing the robber by his hips and lifted him off the ground with a body slam.

When he fell, I was able to grab the gun and shoot two of the three robbers remaining. Before I was able to take out the last robber, I saw my brother throw a two-punch combo to the last guy.

By the time we took out all five of the robbers, we heard the police making their way in. We left before they were able to question us.

DAVID

I heard a knock at my door as soon as I grabbed another slice of pizza. I opened the door thinking it was the delivery person, and I told him, "Look man I do not have any money to tip you."

When I saw who was at my door, I realized it was both Angela and Eric looking tired and out of breath and not the pizza man.

"Oh, sorry about that guys, how was your first spy mission?"

Angela says, "Pizza? Really David?"

I told her the same thing I told myself, "I can't possibly do all this work on an empty stomach, but I have another mission for you guys."

"Okay team, for the next mission I see there is another robbery happening at the Electrical Bank. This bank is one of the tallest banks in the nation. This mission may require you to use those Gripper Gloves Eric."

Eric says, "I look forward to putting these bad boys to use."

"For this next mission there is another team of five gang members plus their boss who calls all the shots. For this task, I will be giving you guys earpieces to listen to my commands. I have the blueprint of the building, and I have access to all the cameras. This way we can at least be one step ahead," I say. "Alright team you all start heading to the next bank location and I'll keep you informed through the earpiece."

When they arrived at the bank, they informed me that the doors had electrical locks that were secured from the inside. This means Eric would have to use his Gripper Gloves to climb up the building a few floors, but not to the top floor where the bank is located.

He was able to get in through the secret vent I have located. Once he made his way inside, I provided him with the code to the electrical lock to be able to let Angela in.

ERIC

I made it inside like a real spy and started making my way to Angela on the first floor and used the code David gave me to let her in.

We headed to the elevator to take these guys out from doing another bank robbery. David informed us that there were two guards heading down to the first floor where we were at.

We positioned ourselves on both sides of the elevator waiting for them to come down. When they reached the first floor, we took out the bank robbers with a single punch. We grabbed their guns and made our way to take out the rest.

When the elevator opened, we shot the two guards. The boss realized two of his men were down.

He tried to shoot us but we dodged his bullets. I did a front roll towards him and did a sweep kick to knock him on the floor.

I shouted, "Angela, use one of your absorb balls."

She quickly pressed the red button and before he was able to get back up, he was suctioned inside the ball.

Two weeks have passed, and the government contacted Eric, David and Angela to give recognition for defeating the ongoing bank robberies.

The conversation led to them asking them if they were willing to travel to Brazil to take down the biggest juggernaut bank robber crew in the nation.

Upon success they will be granted a title of Spies of the Nation and 50 million dollars.

DAVID

Since the offer from the government to take down the juggernaut crew in Brazil, we decided to take on this mission.

We brought weapons, devices and extra snacks for me to stay alert. With our weapons, technology and my hacking skills we took out the bank robbers.

It wasn't an easy defeat since they had master capoeiristas. However, we completed this mission and were granted our reward.

VIOLENCE IS NOT THE KEY

You don't have to choose to be bad.
That thought hit me while driving to the gas station.

As I stepped out of the car, heading toward the store,
I saw someone robbing it.

In my mind I thought:
Why rob a store?
I know work is hard,
But doing wrong doesn't make it right.
Hurting others just for money?
Is that really the best choice?
Is that really who you are?

I closed my eyes.
Took a deep breath.
Felt anger... and sadness.

Then,
I opened my eyes.
Took a step forward,
Power surging through my body,
Veins rising beneath my skin.
The wind rushed against me.

I walked to the door.
Opened it.
Silence... filled my ears.

All eyes locked on me.
But I wasn't embarrassed.
I wasn't scared.
I refused to let fear take control.
I own my mind.
I own my body.

One robber.
Pistol in his right hand.
Dressed in all black.
Gloves tight.
But I stepped closer,
Face to face.

I looked him in the eyes.
He looked confused.
His hands relaxed.
The grip on the gun loosened.

And I spoke.

"Is this what you really want?
Is this where your heart is?
Is this what you need?

Hurting people over a dollar?
Do your loved ones know what you're doing?

We don't need more pain in this world.
We don't need more bad decisions.

Are you scared of being good?
Being kind?
Being better?

If you want to feel important,
Don't bring others down to lift yourself up."

I told him,
"God blessed you to be here,
To do good.
This isn't what we're meant for.
This isn't the lesson kids should witness.
Look around,
See the fear in their eyes.

Is this who you are?"

He stared back at me.
Then dropped the gun.

In his left hand,
A big bag of money.
He walked to the cashier,
Returned every dollar.
Came back to me and said,
"Thank you."

I said,
"You're welcome.
But don't ever make a choice like this again."

He left the store.

I bought some potato chips...
And walked out too.

God gave me the strength
To stand for peace.
To speak with courage.
And to choose what's right.

youthwriterspress.com

A program of Youth Writer's Camp, Inc., Youth Writer's Press exists to create a safe space where young voices are heard, valued, and amplified. We are dedicated to producing and publishing work that allows youth to share their truths with the world. Our mission is to equip the next generation of writers with the resources, confidence, and platform to turn their stories into lasting works that resound far beyond the page.

youthwriterscamp.com

This book was created as part of Youth Writer's Camp, Inc., a nonprofit organization whose mission is to motivate communities to redefine hope for young people through mentoring, enrichment, and creativity.

In our workshops and programs, we blend literacy enrichment, social-emotional development, and creative entrepreneurship — using writing as a tool for healing, growth, and community connection.

Youth Writer's Camp Values:

COURAGE Creating the strength to face challenges with confidence.

RESILIENCE Creating the ability to bounce back and keep moving forward.

EMPATHY Creating connections by truly understanding others' feelings.

AUTHENTICITY Creating a space where you can be your true self without masks.

TRANSPARENCY Creating an atmosphere of openness and honesty, where vulnerability is valued.

ENTERPRISING Creating opportunities through innovation and a dynamic mindset.